JACK and the Beanstalk

retold by Carol North • illustrated by Brenda Dabaghian

GOLDEN PRESS • NEW YORK

Western Publishing Company, Inc., Racine, Wisconsin

nce upon a time there was a boy named
Jack who lived with his mother in a little cottage.
They had barely enough to eat. One day Jack's
mother said to him, "We have no money left to buy
food. You must take the cow to town and sell her."

On the way to town, Jack met a strange little man who offered to buy the cow.

"What will you give me for her?" Jack asked.

The little man reached into his pocket and pulled out a handful of shiny beans. "These," he said. "They're magic!"

Jack could not take his eyes off the beans. "It's a bargain," he said.

And home Jack ran as fast as he could.

"Oh, Mother!" he said.
"See what I got for the cow!"
When his mother saw the beans she was so angry she threw them out the window.
That night Jack went to bed without any supper.

But in the morning, when Jack looked out the window, he was amazed to see a giant beanstalk that seemed to reach all the way to the clouds.

Being a very curious fellow, Jack decided to climb the beanstalk. Up, up, up he went, climbing into the sky.

At last he was above the clouds. There before him stood a gigantic castle. Jack was hungry after his long climb, so he went to the castle door and knocked.

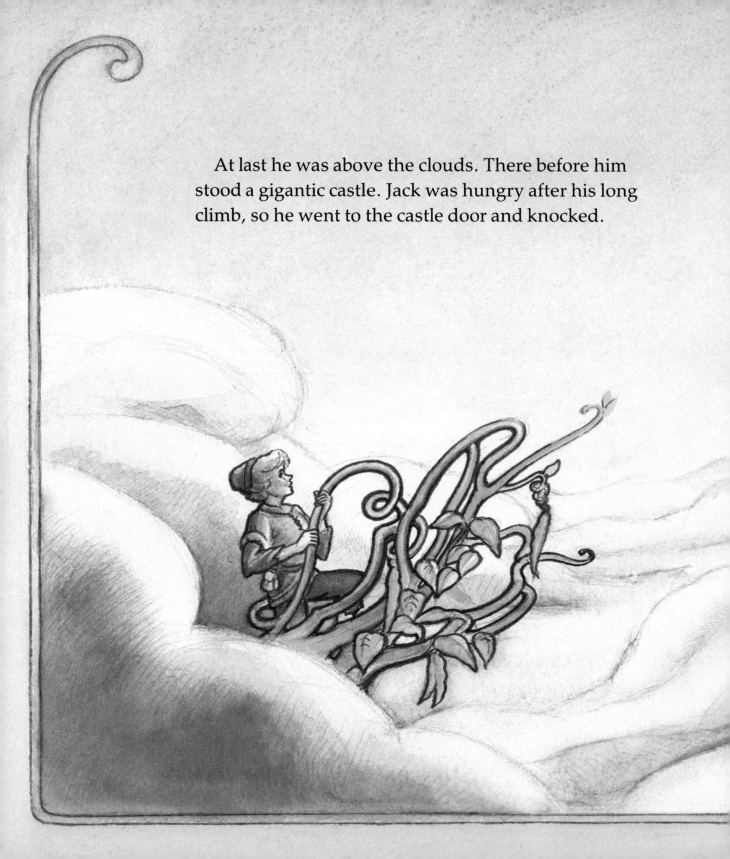

A giant woman opened the door.
"Please ma'am, may I have
something to eat?" asked Jack.
The woman took pity on poor Jack
and led him into her big kitchen.

But just as she gave him a crust of bread, Jack heard the sound of thundering footsteps. The floor began to shake and the walls to tremble.

"Quick," the old woman said to Jack, "get into the oven and hide. My husband is coming."

At that moment a horrible giant came sniffing and snorting into the room. He bellowed:

> *Fee, fie, fo, fum,*
> *I smell the blood of an Englishman.*
> *Be he alive, or be he dead,*
> *I'll grind his bones to make my bread!*

The giant searched all around the kitchen. But when he reached for the oven door, his wife stopped him.

"It's only your supper you smell," she said, and she quickly set before him six roasted pigs. He sat down at the table and ate every one.

When he was through, he called to his wife, "Get me my magic hen." His wife brought in a fine hen.

"Lay!" commanded the giant. And the hen laid a golden egg. "Lay!" he said again to the hen. Once more the hen laid a golden egg.

Jack, peering around the oven door, could not believe his eyes.

At last the giant fell asleep at the table. Jack crept out of the oven and seized the hen. Then away he ran, down the beanstalk, as fast as he could.

"Look what I brought you, Mother!" he cried.

His mother was overjoyed when she found out what the hen could do. "We'll never go hungry again," she said, "for we'll sell the golden eggs in town."

But after a while, Jack began to wonder if there was anything else to be had in the castle.

Being a very curious fellow,
he climbed the magic beanstalk
again and knocked at the castle door.

"Oh, it's you," said the giant's wife. "You dare
not come in—my husband is very cross today."

But Jack persuaded her to give him something to eat.

Just as he was about to take a bite from a large
apple tart, Jack heard the giant's thundering footsteps.
"Quick, hide in the wood box," the old woman said.
The giant came stomping into the kitchen bellowing:

Fee, fie, fo, fum,
I smell the blood of an Englishman.
Be he alive, or be he dead,
I'll grind his bones to make my bread!

The giant looked all around the kitchen and was
about to open the wood box when his wife stopped
him. "It's only your supper you smell," she said, and
she quickly set before him six roasted geese.

He sat down at the table and ate
every one. When he was through,
he called to his wife, "Bring me my magic harp."
    The wife set the harp on the table. "Play,"
the giant commanded the harp. And play it did,
ever so sweetly. Soon the giant was fast asleep
at the table.

Jack jumped out of the
wood box and grabbed
the harp. Then away he ran
as fast as he could.

But the magic harp cried out,
"Master! Master! Wake up!"
The giant staggered to his feet
and took off after Jack in a rage.
Jack reached the beanstalk and
began climbing down.
The giant followed.

On the ground, Jack grabbed a hatchet and chopped the beanstalk in two.

Down it came, giant and all, crashing across the meadow. That was the end of the giant.

As for Jack and his mother, they had a hen that laid golden eggs and a harp that played beautiful music. So they lived happily ever after.